Yellowstone National Park

A Level Three Reader

By Cynthia Klingel and Robert B. Noyed

The Child's World®

On the cover...
This picture shows bison and an elk at the
Firehole River in Yellowstone National Park.

Published by The Child's World®
P.O. Box 326
Chanhassen, MN 55317-0326
800-599-READ
www.childsworld.com

Photo Credits
© 1999 Adam Jones/Dembinsky Photo Assoc. Inc.: 6
© A&L Sinibaldi/Tony Stone Images: 10
© Barbara Filet/Tony Stone Images: 5
© 1994 Bill Lea/Dembinsky Photo Assoc. Inc.: 21
© David Schultz/Tony Stone Worldwide: cover
© 1999 DPA/Dembinsky Photo Assoc. Inc.: 25
© Gary Brettnacher/Tony Stone Worldwide: 29
© James Randklev/Tony Stone Images: 13
© 1999 Mike Barlow/Dembinsky Photo Assoc. Inc.: 22
© Photri. Inc.: 18
© 1999 Scott T. Smith/Dembinsky Photo Assoc. Inc.: 26
© 1993 Stan Osolinski/Dembinsky Photo Assoc. Inc.: 9, 14
© 1999 Stan Osolinski/Dembinsky Photo Assoc. Inc.: 17
© XNR Productions, Inc.: 3

Project Coordination: Editorial Directions, Inc.
Photo Research: Alice K. Flanagan

Library of Congress Cataloging-in-Publication Data
Klingel, Cynthia Fitterer.
Yellowstone National Park / by Cynthia Klingel and Robert B. Noyed.
p. cm. — (Wonder books)
"A level three reader" —Cover.
Summary: Describes Yellowstone National Park, its location, its landscape,
and its scenic wonders, including the Old Faithful geyser.
ISBN 1-56766-828-3 (lib. bdg. : alk. paper)
1. Yellowstone National Park—Juvenile literature.
[1. Yellowstone National Park. 2. National parks and reserves.]
I. Noyed, Robert B.   II. Title.   III. Wonder books (Chanhassen, Minn.)

F722 .K56   2000
978.7'52—dc21   99-057847

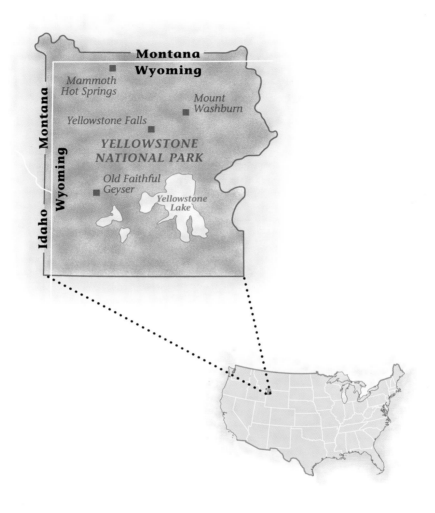

Do you know where Yellowstone National Park is? Here is a map to help you find it.

Yellowstone National Park is the oldest national park in the United States. It became a national park in 1872. Millions of visitors come to the park each year.

These visitors are watching Old Faithful in Yellowstone National Park.

5

Yellowstone is a very large park. It covers more than 2 million acres (810,000 hectares) of land. Almost all of this land remains **wilderness.**

This part of Yellowstone National Park is called Hayden Valley.

Yellowstone is so big that it extends into three states. Most of the park is in northwest Wyoming. Parts of the park are also in southwest Montana and southeast Idaho.

This picture shows a part of the park called Minerva Springs.

Yellowstone is a special park. Nowhere else in the world are there so many different natural wonders. Yellowstone has **canyons**, hot springs, waterfalls, **geysers**, and much more.

This hot spring is in the Wyoming part of Yellowstone.

One of the most famous **sites** at Yellowstone is Old Faithful. Old Faithful is a geyser. A geyser is a hole in the ground that shoots water into the air. Old Faithful shoots water up to 190 feet (58 meters) in the air about every 80 minutes!

From far away, it is easy to see how high Old Faithful shoots water into the air.

Old Faithful is part of the Upper Geyser Basin. This part of the park has several geysers. In fact, there are more geysers here than anywhere else in the world.

This picture shows a rainbow near Castle Geyser in Yellowstone.

Visitors can see many hot springs in Yellowstone. Hot springs are pools of hot water. The water is heated deep in the earth. The water bubbles to the surface and makes a hot pool.

16   This part of Yellowstone is called Beauty Pool.

The Grand Canyon of Yellowstone is a canyon along the Yellowstone River. The canyon is 20 miles (32 kilometers) long. There are many beautiful waterfalls in the canyon.

This waterfall is called Lower Falls.

Hayden Valley is a part of the park that is home to many animals. Grizzly bears live here. Buffalo, elk, **coyotes,** and many birds also live in the valley.

Large grizzly bears like this one live in Yellowstone National Park. →

21

The park has many mountain peaks. Mount Washburn is the park's main mountain peak. Bighorn sheep feed on the mountainside. It is a good place for visitors to hike.

 This bighorn sheep is watching for signs of danger.

The world's largest **petrified forest** is also in the park. A petrified tree is a tree that has turned into stone. This does not happen very often, so the petrified trees at Yellowstone are a very unusual sight.

This is one of Yellowstone's petrified trees. →

25

Yellowstone National Park offers many things for visitors to do. Some people camp in the park. Some people fish in the park's rivers. Many people hike on the trails that run throughout the park.

This boy is fishing along the Firehole River in the Wyoming part of Yellowstone.

Yellowstone National Park is open in the spring, summer, and fall. Only parts of the park are open in the winter. Yellowstone National Park is one of the most popular vacation spots in the United States.

This picture shows an elk as it walks alone at sunrise. →

Glossary

canyons (KAN-yunz)
Canyons are deep, narrow river valleys with high sides.

coyotes (ky-OH-teez)
Coyotes are furry animals that look like small dogs.

geysers (GIE-zerz)
Geysers are holes in the ground that shoot water into the air.

petrified forest (PEH-trih-fyed FOR-est)
A petrified forest has trees with wood that has turned into stone over time.

sites (SITES)
Sites are places where something is found or where something took place.

wilderness (WILL-der-ness)
Wilderness is a land area where no people live.

Index

To Find Out More

Books

Buchheimer, Naomi, and Charles Dougherty (illustrator). *I Know a Ranger.* New York: Putnam, 1971.

Martin, Cyd. *A Yellowstone ABC.* New York: Rinehart, 1992.

Petersen, David. *Yellowstone.* Chicago: Children's Press, 1992.

Web Sites

Visit our homepage for lots of links about Yellowstone National Park:
http://www.childsworld.com/links.html

Note to Parents, Teachers, and Librarians:
We routinely verify our Web links to make sure they're safe, active sites—so encourage your readers to check them out!

Note to Parents and Educators

Welcome to Wonder Books®! These books provide text at three different levels for beginning readers to practice and strengthen their reading skills. Additionally, the use of nonfiction text provides readers the valuable opportunity to *read to learn*, not just to learn to read.

These leveled readers allow children to choose books at their level of reading confidence and performance. Nonfiction Level One books offer beginning readers simple language, word choice, and sentence structure as well as a word list. Nonfiction Level Two books feature slightly more difficult vocabulary, longer sentences, and longer total text. In the back of each Nonfiction Level Two book are an index and a list of books and Web sites for finding out more information. Nonfiction Level Three books continue to extend word choice and length of text. In the back of each Nonfiction Level Three book are a glossary, an index, and a list of books and Web sites for further research.

State and national standards in reading and language arts emphasize using nonfiction at all levels of reading development. Wonder Books® fill the historical void in nonfiction material for primary grade readers with the additional benefit of a leveled text.

About the Authors

Cynthia Klingel has worked as a high school English teacher and an elementary school teacher. She is currently the curriculum director for a Minnesota school district. Cynthia lives with her family in Mankato, Minnesota.

Robert B. Noyed started his career as a newspaper reporter. Since then, he has worked in school communications and public relations at the state and national level. Robert lives with his family in Brooklyn Center, Minnesota.